P9-DFK-086

MR. DARCY'S
NIGHT BEFORE
CHRISTMAS

JULIE PETERSEN

ILLUSTRATED BY
SHERYL DICKERT

GIBBS SMITH
TO ENRICH AND INSPIRE HUMANKIND

'Twas the night before Christmas,
    and at Pemberley
Not a servant was stirring;
    they slept peacefully.
A cold snow lay heavy
    all over the park,
While inside, Mr. Darcy
    sat alone in the dark.

He stared at the fire
  and heard the wind blow.
From outside there echoed
  a loud "Ho, ho, ho!"
He heard jingling bells and
  a light prancing hoof,
Why, yes! It was Santa, on top
  of his roof!

F irst down the chimney
    came one big black boot,
And then came old Santa
    all covered in soot.
"Mr. Darcy," he said,
    as he grinned ear to ear,
"Come, tell your friend Santa
    what you'd like this year."

Now, Darcy gave pause:
   his thoughts were a'swirling—
With flashes of fine eyes,
   and ballrooms, and twirling—
Miss Elizabeth Bennet,
   far off at Longbourn . . .
As his mind turned to her,
   he felt very forlorn.

" I have a large fortune
   and quite a good life,
But, as a man single,
   I'm in want of a wife.
There is a young woman
   who's sparked my interest,
Though I doubt, for my status,
   that she is the best."

Santa furrowed his brow
   and he stroked his white beard.
Darcy's great pride was much worse
   than he'd feared.
What could he do
   so proud Darcy would know
That obeying his heart
   was the best way to go?

Inspiration struck Santa;
  he chuckled inside.
"Mr. Darcy," said he,
    "let us go for a ride.
You can help me fill stockings
    on this Christmas night.
And maybe we'll find a Mrs. Darcy—
    all right?"

M r. Darcy agreed and
they sprang to the sleigh.
With a snap of the reins
they were up and away.
They took to the sky through
the stars and the dark
To the county of Kent, and
the grand Rosings Park.

There dwelt Darcy's aunt and
  his sickly cousin, Anne.
When infants, their marriage had
  been his aunt's plan.
Darcy politely but sternly
  rejected this notion.
"I won't marry my cousin
  for all the fish in the ocean!"

"Despite my aunt's attempts,
   this I cannot do.
Please, let us move on."
   And so off they flew.
In London, at the home of the
   Bingleys they stopped,
And down the chimney Santa
   and Mr. Darcy dropped.

"Charles is a fine friend,
   congenial to all,"
said Darcy, "But he's been subdued
   since this fall."
"Perhaps that's because you said
   Jane doesn't care.
But, trust me," said Santa,
   "I know you're wrong there.

"Miss Caroline Bingley," asked Santa,
   "Would she do?"
"No," replied Darcy, "She's too rude
   and a shrew.
I know she is closer to my
   life and high station,
But her attentions to me are
   a source of vexation."

"Very well," replied Santa. "She's all wrong for you. Now, quick, fill these stockings; there's a lot left to do!" They took off once more through wintry London town, And in front of an orphanage, landed back down.

They softly tiptoed 'tween the
  rows of small beds
While the orphan children rested
  their wee little heads.
Santa filled all their stockings while
  Darcy trimmed the tree.
He imagined their faces filled
  with wonder and glee.

Mr. Darcy felt cheer
welling up in his heart,
Perceiving it's not what
you get, but impart.
We must truly love despite
fortune or station,
And show kindness and concern
for all of creation.

At this realization, he paused
and he pondered.
"Why am I so stubborn?"
he silently wondered.
And turning to Santa, he knew
what he wanted.
He was willing to take on that
challenge, undaunted.

"Oh, Santa, I think you know the
 wife I desire,
Let's proceed with all haste into
 far Herefordshire."
And again through the heavens the
 sleigh took its flight
Until the estate of
 Longbourn was in sight.

P eeking out from the chimney
they saw, still, one light shone.
"Look there," whispered Santa, "I
fear we're not alone."
In front of the fire, with her
feet all tucked under,
Miss Elizabeth Bennet
lay sweetly in slumber.

Santa chuckled, "Though you thought her to be tolerable only,
Without her quick wit, you would surely be lonely.
You now find her handsome and tempting enough,
But winning her heart may prove yet a bit tough.

She's seen your disdain and has heard Wickham's slander.
Tell her the truth about him with the utmost of candor.
Now I'll wake her quite gently and give aid to your cause."
So Elizabeth woke to the face of Santa Claus.

But soon she spied Darcy
   peeking out from behind.
Her eyes narrowed, brow furrowed—
   was she out of her mind?
This man whose harsh words had
   caused Bingley to flee—
What on earth was he doing
   by her Christmas tree?!

"My dear Elizabeth," said Santa.
   "I can see you're distressed.
We don't mean to startle.
   Darcy is here as my guest.
Please listen to him and
   he may calm your fears.
Wickham's on my naughty list—
   and has been for years."

"Yes, Darcy's proud, but his deeds have been good.
I'd say he is quite a fine man
—indeed I would."
This pronouncement Elizabeth's fears did relieve,
For if you can't trust Santa,
who can you believe?

Mr. Darcy then knelt,
　　for he knew what to do.
"Miss Elizabeth," he said,
　　"I ardently love you.
I know this is fast, and we've
　　borne our share of strife,
But please do me the honor of
　　becoming my wife."

"I have learned that what matters
  is not status and rank,
And for that I have you, my dear,
  and Santa to thank.
Please forgive the ungentlemanly
  things that I've said,
And let us make plans for our
  future ahead."

Elizabeth smiled and then
    nodded approbation.
She could feel that Mr. Darcy
    spoke with great admiration.
And Santa was glad that his
    lesson, well taught,
Had changed Darcy's heart;
    his old ways now forgot.

S anta left the two right there,
  beneath the mistletoe,
Finished filling stockings and
  made ready to go.
Up the chimney he rose,
  and gave the reins a swish,
Glad to help Darcy get
  his best Christmas wish.

The two at the window were
waving farewell,
As the church started chiming its first
Christmas bells.
Then they heard Santa call,
as he flew out of sight,
"Happy Christmas to all,
and to all a good night!"

First Edition
19 18 17 16   5 4 3 2

Published by
Gibbs Smith
P.O. Box 667
Layton, Utah 84041

1.800.835.4993 orders
www.gibbs-smith.com

Designed and illustrated by Sheryl Dickert
Printed and bound in China
Gibbs Smith books are printed on either recycled,
100% post-consumer waste, FSC-certified papers
or on paper produced from sustainable PEFC-
certified forest/controlled wood source. Learn
more at www.pefc.org.

Library of Congress Cataloging-in-Publication Data

Petersen, Julie, author.
  Mr. Darcy's Night Before Christmas / Julie
Petersen ; illustrated by Sheryl Dickert. —
First edition.
     pages cm
  ISBN 978-1-4236-3797-4
1. Christmas poetry. 2. Darcy, Fitzwilliam
(Fictitious character)—Poetry. 3. American wit and
humor. 4. Santa Claus—Poetry. I. Dickert, Sheryl,
illustrator. II. Moore, Clement Clarke, 1779-1863.
Night before Christmas. III. Title.
  PS3616.E84259M7 2015
  811'.6—dc23
                              2015003585